"Into My Arms is a startling portal into Estelle Phillips' daring imagination, a formally inventive freefall into myth and possibility wherein the story of a man in a glider dropping from the sky interweaves with visions of a translucent horse, wise trees, mourning widows and the graveyard voices of the deceased, recalling perhaps the 'Tibetan Book of the Dead', Alice Oswald's 'Dart', George Saunders' 'Lincoln in the Bardo' and the Mabinogion. But you can't pin it down, it's its own strange thing and it's told with breathtaking audacity. Another triumph for the small yet mighty Road Song Books..."

Jeff Young, 2025 TLS Ackerley Prize winner for Wild Twin

"A lyrical evocation of the inner life of trees and their relationship with one family through times of love, loss and wonder..."

Angela McAllister, author of An Ocean Full of Stories

"Estelle Phillips' vision is deep and poetic..."

Paul Wood, writer of Tree Hunting

"An amazing tour-de-force – a moving story..."

Tim Craven, The Arborealists

"In order to save nature, we must re-enchant it. Estelle Phillips does just this with Into My Arms. Her writing harks back to a time when nature hummed and thrummed with a vibrancy and a magic that we struggle to fathom these days..."

Ben Goldsmith, Rewilding the World podcast,
and writer of God is an Octopus

"Something deliciously wicked this way comes. Estelle Phillips' Into My Arms is a staggering achievement. Fearless writing to shout about..."

Mark McDonald, The Observer

"A poetic scrapbook of memories and family history. Dramatic exchanges, newspaper cuttings, sentient trees, and ancient connections. The dialogue between past and present, plant and planet, down the years. Ghostly figures, tricksy thermals and powerless falling from unpowered flight. A miracle, a promise long kept..."

David Gladwin, author of Coldwell

"Why trees matter, hidden histories, and memories of the natural world. Reflective, mysterious and intriguing..."

Mark Wigan, artist and writer of Drawing the Night

"Never before have I seen nature and words so perfectly blended. Estelle has created a vision in the reader's mind. Taking them by the hand, walking them through beautifully crafted storytelling full of myths, legends and folklore tinged with reality, fused together seamlessly..."

Nat Wood Fox, writer and screenwriter

"Into My Arms exists beyond the frontiers of modern fiction writing. This ethereal gathering of countryside tales enthralls at every turn. Simply beautiful..."

Alan Edward Roberts, author of Gentle November and Cerberus

Road Song Books, England, UK

Typeset in EB Garamond

Into My Arms

Produced and project managed by Alan Edward Roberts | Edited by Alan Edward Roberts and Matthew Usher

Design by Chris Ranken | Illustrations by Rose Roberts | Publicity by Alan Edward Roberts and Cat Tickell

Website and tech support: Federation Design (Cambridgeshire)

ISBN: 978-1-9160833-5-6

A CIP catalogue record is available from the British Library

www.roadsongbooks.com

Printed and bound in Great Britain by Clays Ltd, Elcograf S.p.A.

Into My Arms

by

Estelle Phillips

www.roadsongbooks.com

Also by Estelle Phillips

Poetry

Motherhoodlum

The Headless Horseman

Estelle Phillips is a writer and performance poet. She lives in Wiltshire with her dog. She is the winner of BBC Radio Wiltshire's Ten Tiny Plays About Wiltshire (with *In Memory of Annie*) and Touchnote's Fill The Space (with *Diary of A Panettone*). Her novel *Hard Wet Sand* was runner-up in the Yeovil Literary Prize. Estelle was a member of the 2024/25 Literary Works cohort of emerging writers.

Previous publications include: *Motherhoodlum* (Jawbone Collective) and *The Headless Horseman* (Cranborne Chase National Landscape/Chase & Chalke Landscape Partnership). Her poetry, including *Hand of Hazard*, *Hurricane Lorenzo*, *The Welshman* and *A Lover's Confession*, has appeared in The International Times, Steel Jackdaw, Motherlore and Kingfisher USA.

Estelle's short fiction has appeared in the UK in The New Blackmore Vale Magazine and in US publications including Rock and a Hard Place, Dark Yonder and Jerry Jazz Musician. Pieces include *The Orphaned Fawn*, *Isaac Gulliver's Buzzard*, *Tenderness*, *Twenty-Nine Turquoise Beads* and *Sketch In 'D' Minor*.

Non-fiction including *Hardy's Knuckles*, *The Trapped Doe* and *110 mph – Ten Years In Waiting* have been published in The Clearing, The New Blackmore Vale Magazine and Dialect respectively.

Estelle is a slam winner and has performed at Southbank, the Royal Albert Hall and Chalke Festival. Her journalism includes articles for The Independent and THE, and she is the author of two academic papers.

Estelle hosts the podcast Nature Talks With Humans.

For my grandmother, Jessie

Groom-to-be Killed in Road Crash

Wiltshire Times | 11 May 1938

On Saturday 7 May, shortly after 1.35 p.m. the motor vehicle of Captain William Taylor collided with a wall as he approached Hindon. A witness observed Captain Taylor lose control of his Humber Snipe after he swerved to avoid a pheasant.

Captain Taylor was driving to the Church of St. John the Baptist at Hindon where his marriage to Miss. Jessie Thomas of Chicklade was due to take place.

Our deepest condolences to Miss. Thomas and family and friends of Captain Taylor.

The Bride

The florist caused a commotion in the orchard.

Each tree jostled its best blossom forward
and quivered the veined pink tip of their petals
"Choose me! Choose me!"

The bee danced close to the florist's fingers
suggesting the Gala. She had a soft spot
for the aromatic tree. Despite his vanity
he meant well
and was easily disappointed.
The other trees knew he wished
his flowers to have pride of place
on Jessie's head table.
There was an unspoken agreement, this was best.

The florist shooed the bee away
and chose other trees.
Snip, snip, snip!
Secateurs cut twigs to their quicks.
All the trees were brave
except Gala who shed sappy tears.

The big day dawned warm.
The bee started early,
swerved around the front of the house
and lured by the scent of Gertrude Jekyll
                    in a posy,
                    in a vase,
                    on a linen dressed table,
flew through a half open window,
buzzed past jars of apple blossom
and dived into the pink corolla of a rose.
As she whirred her wings and stuck out her proboscis

a hand stretched over the linen, grasped
the neck of the vase
and removed it

to the dark
of the boot room.
The jars of blossom followed the roses
and the bee buzzed over the table
in a shrinking figure of eight.
Her drone tightened to a whine of confusion.
She tried to retrace the way she came,
banged into a windowpane
and fell to the carpet.

The trees waited all morning.
Leaves turned up and roots firmly down
they chatted excitedly in the sun.
Jessie did not come

to say goodbye.

By 2 o'clock, the trees were quiet.
Their arms sagged,
leaves wilted
and severed fingers drooped to earth.
"We'll never see her again,"

Gala's voice quavered like a viola
and the other trees did not accuse him
of being dramatic.
Each was lost in memories

of Jessie chasing butterflies
and skipping through their trunks.
Running her hands over their bark
"Ring a ring of roses..."
and dressing their limbs with daisy chains
"...a pocketful of posies."
"Of course we will," Wise Bramley growled
and the lopsided swing hung from his bough
jerked as he swallowed a sob.
"They will come together," Russet interjected
and the orchard silenced
in contemplation.
Gala rejoined, "How she laughed
when she atishooed and threw her face to the sky!"
The trees swayed in reverie
and dappled shadows
swung over grass

confusing the bee as she swooped between canopies.
Still drowsy from the bump to her head
she landed heavily on a Gala petal
and took long draughts of nectar
before imparting,
"The blossom is gone."
Revived, she waggled her tail,
shook her antennae
and buzzed off.

"Gone, gone where?"
"What does it mean?"
"Ssshh!" said Bramley, "someone's coming."
The trees twisted their trunks
and skewed their heads to look.
"Act normally," he chided.

Jessie's hair was threaded with daisies
and tears glistened her cheeks.
She stepped softly on moss
that gave to her tread
and her sadness flattened its mounds.

She followed the path to Bramley,
placed her cheek on his nobbled bark
and stroked a scar where an arm was lopped off
to make room for her swing.
It pained the tree
to feel her hurt.
He soothed a lullaby with his leaves
until she lay in the grass at his feet

and cried

herself to sleep.
The trees knitted their branches over her head
and when her breath was deep
dropped delicate petals
white and pink

confetti on her skin.

Tree of Life I

Jessie mourns at William's grave

Jessie **William**

William, I shiver.

Come near, I am warm.

Near how? You are buried.

I remember our walks
on the downs. We held hands

and our blood pulsed in time
through our skin.

Lay your hands
on the land,

dirt grits my fingers

my heart beats
through soil,

and you waltz
in my palms.

This is my earth song
beginning.

Jessie, listen!

I want you
to dance
with someone who lives.

One, two, three,
step, step, close,
one, two, three...

Birth Announcement

Wiltshire Times | 15 November 1944

Mr. and Mrs. Herbert Phillips announce the birth of a baby boy at Salisbury Hospital. The mother was formerly Miss. Jessie Thomas of Chicklade.

Tree of Life II

Jessie presents her newborn at William's grave

Jessie | **William**

William, are you there?

Yes! I heard you step
up the lane
and scrunch gravel.
It's been a while,
were you dancing?

I was. There is someone
I'd like you to meet.

A graveyard 'social.'
How novel!

My son
born three months ago.

I am honoured.
What do you call him?

Derek.

Aah, "To tread with the feet,"
how apt.

He has your eyes.

What does he like?

To frog kick in dappled shade
of the orchard. He grabs
Bramley's branches
and the old tree jigs his twigs
just to hear Derek's baby
belly laugh.

Congratulations, Jessie
you have a 'sapling son.'
I will spread word.
Elder Yew will be pleased
for she has overseen a spate
of fresh graves
and births cheer her up.

You may trust
the family of trees
with Derek's life.

Deaths

Wiltshire Times | 8 July 1968

PHILLIPS, Herbert – On Thursday 4 July 1968 (suddenly). Herbert, beloved husband of Jessie and adoring father of Derek, "He will always be in our hearts."

Tree of Life III

Jessie grieves at Herbert's grave

Jessie	**Herbert**
Herbert, you too are gone.	
	I am sorry.
	How are you, Darling?
I sink in sadness.	
	Do not sink, swim! Swim like an otter.
My will to live wanes.	
	I would have outstayed your end but
your heart gave out and I was not there to save you.	
	There was nothing to be done. How is Derek?
Bereft but Anne comforts him.	

She is a fine
woman for our son.

I wish I were with you.

I do not.
Darling, life goes on

empty
and pointless.

No. There is
much you must do.
I heard on the rootvine
the gamekeeper's
bitch had a litter
and rejected the runt,
a sweet dog with soulful eyes.

Oh no!
A puppy abandoned
for his size.
What will they do?

You know what
gamekeepers are like,
hearts of steel.

Bless you my
Darling, I must go.
I hope you will
come again, soon.

Good-bye, Herbert,
good-bye.

Local Bronze Age Warrior Appears

Wiltshire Times | 1 September 1968

Two days ago, the Bronze Age warrior of Bottlebrush Down presented himself to Mrs. Jessie Phillips as she walked her dog by the tumulus. The warrior rode towards her but vanished when a tractor came into view.

Mrs. Phillips' sighting was thirty years to the day since the eminent archaeologist Dr. Clay saw the spectre. At the time of his sighting, Dr. Clay was driving home to Fovant and the horseman followed him along "for more than a hundred yards" before disappearing into the side of a barrow.

The Headless Horseman

Jessie

"Cuck-oo, cuck-oo!"
I woke and reached for his arm.
The bed beside me was vacant,
his pillow plump.

Loss riddled my bones.
I yearned for the scream of wind in my hair,
rain on my skin,
pulse numbing cold

and took to the downs,
lugged memories along deer tracks.
Hawthorn scratched my clothes
and nettles stung exposed shins.

Three does watched from the middle of the field
and a hare zig-zagged away.
I stumbled through ruts to the highest tumulus
where we used to stand
admiring the sunset
stretch trees over fields.

There, I wept
                        at the edge
                                        of life

and buried our memories under my feet.

It became my weekly habit to sit on the tumulus.
Often I fancied thuds echoed beneath
like bones uncrossing themselves.
I put this down to grief.

One late summer evening on my way to our tumulus
I met a couple on the footpath.
Their plimsolls were clean
and the woman's handbag was hitched on her shoulder

as if she had been shopping.
I accelerated past them, eyes down
counting flint among stones
but as we crossed,
"Err, excuse us..."
"Hello."
"Sorry to disturb your walk,
we're looking for Bottlebrush Down
where the headless horseman was spotted."
"Left at the road and second path right
to the copse on the hill...
is he friendly?"
Man and woman exchanged a look
and the man cleared his throat,
"Well... no, I wouldn't say he was friendly."
"So, if I see him, I can't pat his horse?"
"I wouldn't do that! He's best left alone."
"Thanks for the warning. Good luck, I hope you find him."

Back home, I researched the headless horseman.
A warrior, he won the love of the clan leader's daughter,

returned from a raid,
laid his head on her breast
and heard her heart murmur.
He cured her affliction with foxglove
and the pair's union was blessed

until a rival cited wizardry
for his knowledge of botany,
had the warrior cast from the clan
and decapitated
in an ambush.
The warrior's bones were dumped
in a half-dug tumulus
and the head left
where it fell.

The warrior's ghost rampaged the downs for vengeance.

My weekly vigils continued.
Autumn passed and winter set in.
Long grass dried and snapped,
foliage died back from the deer track

and bare soil revealed old mysteries.
Rain had been heavy when I squelched through mud,
slipped as a thief from bush to bush
and leant on a slender thorned arm which bent,
tumbling me into nettles.
I put my hand on a tussock to push myself up,
received a hard shock to my palm
and scrabbled up under the steady gaze
of three does. Their look was expectant.
To my left a hare squatted on haunches
and stared.
A kite soared overhead
and distant clanking
came from the tumulus.

Alarmed, I turned for home.
The does stepped forward,
the hare's nose twitched
and the kite swooped low
in general request.

I started to walk.

The does advanced three steps
and stamped their delicate hooves,
the hare flicked his ears back and clawed at the grass.
The kite dived at my chest.

I crouched.
The clanking increased,
vibrated underground
to my feet. I put my hand where notes rang
and followed the trail of their beat to the tussock.
Again, my palm found a hard surface.
Shrivelled blades pulled apart to reveal
white too smooth for chalk

and when the object was cleared
I knew it had been lost
for a very long time.
Breathing heavily
I sat back on my thighs
and prayed,
"God rest his soul."

The does, the hare and the kite watched and waited.

I leant forward and examined the skull.
Charred edges of sockets were full of pink cyclamen,
their petals welcomed the wintry sunshine
and stripy snails crept through a jaw
scorched by fire.
Moss greened over cracks in bone fractured
by a blow to the back of the head.
A labyrinth spider scurried up one nostril
and both holes were darkened by smoke
as if the head simmered with revenge
when it landed, blackened the grass
to warn creatures away.

Over the years, rain cooled the skull's rage.
It learnt to see passing clouds and seasons.
Blades stroked its bone as they grew.
The skull took pleasure in the patter of rain on its crown,
wind blowing on its hollowed cheeks
and sighing through its earholes.
The hedgehogs took pity and mooted the idea

of rolling it to the tumulus to join its bones.
Embedded at its base the skull would not shift.
They asked the moles to help.
The skull was too big to pass through their tunnels.
It remained hidden

increasingly lonely.
When animals approached
the skull did its best to be appealing
by keeping its jaw still and catching the sun in its cheeks.

Centuries of nature softened its need for revenge.
One summer a harvest mouse nested in a socket;
one eyed, the skull watched corn ripen
trying not to giggle when pups crawled in its
head and tickled.

The skull rested comfortably in my hands.
Snails and spiders clung on, not wanting to leave
and I carried it to the tumulus.
The does, hare and kite followed.
As we neared the clanking intensified.

Turf shook as I climbed to the top
and laid the skull where I usually sat.

Out of respect for bodily reunion
I turned for home.
The does faded into the forest,
the hare settled into his nest
and the kite swept down the valley.

The next week I went to the tumulus.
Its top had been ripped open
and the skull was gone.
My hopes for a sighting were high.
Despite a long walk and dallied hours
I did not see the skeleton.

Morose, I headed for home.
Thunder rumbled from a cloudless sky.
I turned up my collar and quickened my pace.
Thunder continued from the west.
I trekked the path through a copse of beech
to the ghost hunters' crossroads.

Rumbles loudened.
Not thunder but hooves galloping.
I swung round.
A dot glowed between trunks.
Thunder banged in my ears.
The dot enlarged,
became a steed charging the path at me.
Seventeen hands of see-through sinew and bone
in luminescent skin,
his shoulders flexed with power.
Legs folded and unfolded in rhythmic skim over earth
but the sound was tremendous.
On his back a horseman shimmered
through hanging boughs without hindrance
swinging a ball and chain over his head.
No saddle separated beast from man
who balanced with a translucent hand on the wither.
As one they descended through trees,
hair and mane poured behind
and earth sprung like the skin of a drum
in time with the horse's hooves.
The springs leapt higher with each tree they passed.

Rigid with fear, I froze.

Horse and rider were three trees off when
air sucked away.
Feathered hooves skidded to a stop,
the horse arched his neck in a Lipizzaner bow
and I saw buttercups
garlanded his forelock.
The horse reared
and I stole a glance at the rider.
Buttercups burnished a scar round his neck
and his sockets shone gold
with years of sun.
The warrior swivelled his head at me
and grimaced a smile with his jaw.
Snails chorused tentacles from his teeth.
He swung his ball and chain,
deftly severed a twig from a beech tree.
bent over his horse
and handed it to me
with a meaningful look.
The twig quivered like a wand in my fingers.

The stallion snorted and pawed the ground.
The warrior tilted his head
and in a pirouette
they were gone,

running in the wind.

I planted the twig on the tumulus.
It grew into a fine Copper Beech
whose roots embrace our memories.
I sit at its feet. On windy days
the trunk sways
in my spine.

Does bring their fawns to the tumulus for grazing,
hares skip over the grass for fun
and kites pass low, hunting.
Every spring a cuckoo calls

and I reach for his arm.

Salisbury Solicitor Competes in Gliding Championships

Wiltshire Times | 26 May 1987

Local solicitor Derek Phillips has qualified to compete in the Gliding Championships next month at Lasham Airfield in Hampshire.

Mr. Phillips is known locally for his vigorous defence of the New Age Travellers in Stonehenge's 'Battle of the Beanfield.' He is the son of Jessie Phillips of Chicklade, archivist of historic records for Bottlebrush Down.

No doubt his wife, Anne and the couple's three children will be cheering from the runway. We look forward to reporting back on his progress.

Good luck Mr. Phillips!

Into My Arms

Brother Beech **Derek Phillips**

When Elder Yew Tree saw them,
her needles hackled on raised veins
and bark scales purpled.
Immediately she sent word,
"They are coming."

Giant white birds
sliced through sky
in silence. They did not honk
across their wings,
take turns to lead
but travelled straight
as arrows fired by Ares.

They started as many,

It wasn't a very good gliding day
but I'd had a successful first leg

and then we had to go back up
in a north easterly direction.
But conditions were bad
for soaring.
The thermals were weak and broken.
You had to fight to make progress.

a flock of stiff winged raptors
shivering angular shadows
on land beneath.
Trees froze
as they passed overhead,
not wanting to be seen
as a perch
for their wings would sever our limbs
if they landed in us
and claws were concealed
in sleek bellies. We imagined
their talons ripping our cork
and winced at the thought.

There were three or four other gliders
apart from myself,
spread out.
Each looking at each other
and I remember
feeling

this was like it would have been in the
Second World War coming back from a
successful mission... We were all a similar
sort of age so we would have grown up
when the war was about us.

There it was, on the second leg.
And I was keeping up
with these people
who were no doubt
quite a bit better than me.
I went over the River Thames
and headed for the second turn point.
Conditions were getting worse,

less
and less
lift.

My object was
to get round the turn
and establish myself
on the final glide to Lasham.
I wouldn't be first,
I wouldn't be second
but I wouldn't be as far down as tenth.
It would be a good result.

I came to an area
where there were ups
and downs, you know.
And there was woodland,
trees about.

It was said that hot cumuli
deflected their course
and the hotter the air
the more they liked it.
Single eyed, the giants soared
upward like eagles
I'd seen rise through cirrus on a hot day.
Ash Tree suggested
their feathers would melt
and my sisters clapped their knotted boughs

in derision for Ash Tree had predicted rain
in the summer of seventy-six.

The sun reached its zenith.
Our leaves curled with thirst.
We drooped
in air thick with clicks and pops
and pheromones of other trees
raising Elder Yew's concern to alarm:
the giants were coming our way.

I was not scared
though I am alone on the ridge.
A 'miracle sapling'
I was not expected to survive
this far from my colony.
My mother sustained me

before she was felled.
Her dismembered parts
were left to rot in a heap
until the tractor came.
I was ten.
My sisters brought me up.
Seventy-five years older than me
they stand as a copse
in a sheltered dell
and are overprotective.

My view is a knuckled valley
split by a river
that sings as it sweeps to sea.
At dusk I sway in time

with its slips, slides and gurgles
and the birds in my leaves go to sleep.

The world rotated into afternoon.
In a cooler sky
grey strata replaced cumuli.
The blackbird flew from me
and foraged for supper.
Sparrows fidgeted to my fingertips,
launched skyward
and swooped to a spill of corn.
Jenny Wren bobbled from sprig to sprig
looking for spiders.
Her claws tickled my bark. I laughed
and my sisters frowned.
They think I indulge the bird.
I do not heed their disapproval
for Wren is my friend.

I am solitary but not lonely.

A report arrived from Willow Tree
on the bank of River Thames.
Her minty breath described
predators circling.

I was not very fast
not very high
probably about eighteen hundred feet
above the ground, possibly lower,
well, it would have been lower.

There were one or two other gliders
close by me
so I persevered, tried to keep up
but the other gliders
were better performance gliders
which survive marginal conditions
rather better than one's own

and I don't think
I took a lot of notice of that.

Their wings glinted like knives in the sun
and cruel blades glittered water's skin.
Willow submerged her forearms,
sank her feet in the riverbank
and made herself as small as she could.
Tears welled from her nodes,
dripped into the river
and splashed haloes
through the giants' reflections.
Her fear shot through sky to Hawthorn,
zipped down hedges, into the orchard
and lit to Sycamore
who oversees the dell
where my sisters grow.
He huffed his leaves
and flexed his skewed boughs
but was not perturbed

until the news,
the giants were coming our way!

I was going slower and slower
to try and keep up, not to lose altitude
s l o w e r and s l o w e r
which was actually going beyond

a safe thing for me

but it was still safe enough
for the glider which was closest to me.

A bulletin quickly followed:
a giant bird had dropped from the sky
and landed in stubble. It opened its eye
and a man climbed from its pupil,
walked rows of shorn corn
and a mile down the road for help.
More humans came,
dismantled the bird wing by wing,
loaded it into a coffin
and drove off.
Opinion ricocheted
between Elder Yew and Sycamore.
Hills and dales cringed
beneath their dissent.
Even Copper Beech

of the far tumulus joined in.
Until Sycamore pronounced

these were not birds
but humans
playing wind with false wings.
His judgment was questioned
by ranks of Fir
who suffer at the teeth of a saw

but I believed Sycamore.
He is like an uncle to me.
I was a whippersnapper
when an elephant trunk tornado
breached the horizon.
Animals and plants cowered
as she traversed fields,
whipped insects and foliage into a spin,
tore leaves from plants
and discarded them
with malicious abandon.
Sycamore witnessed the tornado
fix her eye on me.
She gyrated in my direction.
He interrupted her hiss
with a series of clicks.
Affronted, the funnel turned on him.
As she neared he set green helicopters free.

They played her like a summer breeze
and teased her angry squall.
Humiliated, she lunged at him.
Sycamore took his chance,
enveloped her in his canopy.
Enraged, she forked lightning
into his spread, ripped off his limbs
and tossed them to the ground.
Sycamore tightened his grip
and squeezed like a python.
The tornado howled and shrieked,
spat hailstones at his leaves.
My sisters and I watched him quiver
and strain at his roots.
He lifted from earth in a spray of dirt.
A crack rent the air
and fissures ruptured
the ground around him.
He pitched.

My sisters covered their eyes.

Mesmerized, I watched
his vascular tissue bulge.
His bark peeled off and fell
to his feet among shredded leaves.
The tornado screeched like a witch
and accelerated.

Sycamore stretched. His roots
and exposed filaments straightened.

I thought he would relinquish his grip.
Instead, he sacrificed
his trunk
to the spin, wrestled
her rage into his stem
and down his veins,

buried it in dirt.

Afterwards, my sisters thought
he would slowly die.
But I had seen him musculate
wood from wind
and trusted his strength.
Since that day his limbs contort

and he slants
on a twisted stem.
Sycamore is marked
victorious.

My sisters bustled their oval leaves
"We said it was human!"
I did not point out
they said nothing of the sort

and Sycamore bristled with indignation.
His sap began to rise
but he was distracted
by two men
who entered the valley with guns.

Down below there was a field
with some people, I don't know
if they were poaching
or something like that.

By then I suppose I'd been flying
three hours fairly concentrated
and lacking water.
Probably come to think of it now,
dehydrated

and my speed went
s l o w e r.

I saw the blackbird had eaten his fill
but chose not to come home to me
and roosted in Sister Seven Beech.
The sparrows too were sated
and began their return
but diverted to Sister Three.
A quarrel broke out
with Three's resident sparrows

and my sisters demanded
I call my birds back. I did,
but the sparrows preened their wings
and wiped their beaks,
selectively deaf.
My sisters flounced their heads
in irritation

Gently gliding
s l o w e r

until a shadow slipped over them.
Motionless, they glowered at me.
After it passed, they huddled
with their backs to me,
twigs knitted
to stop their thoughts escaping
up the scarp
to me on the ridge.
They whispered
and nodded
in urgent agreement.

The shadow glided towards me.
My sisters' leaves stood on end.
As one they messaged me,
"Freeze."

I held myself perfectly still
and urged Wren to do the same.

gently, gently gliding
beyond a safe thing for me
s l o w e r

The shadow carved over me.
Though I trembled,
Wren hopped up and down my trunk
searching for supper.
Rigid with anxiety
and their disagreement forgotten,
my sisters conferred with Sycamore.
They folded their leaves
over their pheromones
to keep their discussion private.
But green leaves are unruly
and prone to rebel; they
release pheromones
if tempted
by a breeze.
And my sisters have no control over the wind.
A gust blew from their copse to me.
Laden with pheromones
the gust slowed
as it slithered through my branches.
My sisters' scent of distress

clung to my twigs.
My fingers twitched
and my roots itched in chalk
which is normally comfortable.

until the glider lost all speed

and suddenly

flipped!

Instead of me sitting there gliding

whoaaaargh!

I was looking through
the screen
at the land below.

Instead of trees being a trunk
with a top to it
all I saw were green circles

the glider was
dropping

Again, the shadow passed over me.
This time it went the other way.
I asked my sisters,
"Is it dangerous?"
Their reply came straight away,
"Don't talk."

and
down you go

A chill shook my bole.
Wren leant her body
to mine. Her tiny heart
pattered into my wood.

and
down it was going

Air messed my head,
jagged my top leaves
this way and that

and turning.

It was quite beyond me to recover
from this spin
and I said, "What a bloody mess!"

Because there I was doing very well
in the competition

and now I was crashing

without proper insurance for the
glider or myself and a wife and three
children to think about.

My mind was full of preoccupations.

And the thought of even trying to
rectify the stall... I was only about
fifteen hundred feet up and I'd be down in the
ground in no time. Some aces, well
Ralph Jones, could have come out
of that all right

but I was going in

and knew I was going in.

Apart from the other things in my
mind was the fact that I was going to
crash into that tree

because I was going round
and round

over one tree in particular,

beautifully circular.

and the shadow passed again.
Sharp edges
stoked memory of what befell
my forbears in the Great War.
I juddered
from the points of my leaves
to my toes.
My sisters glared
and I knew their anger to be love.

I did my best to not move

but the shadow passed

enlarged, swinging

left

to

right.

Air squashed and parted my leaves.
I shuddered and couldn't help myself,
cried out to my sisters,
"I'm trying!"

They shouted back
"Sycamore says
it's a human wind machine
falling down."

It was waiting for me.

It was headed straight for me
but I was confident I could brush it off
and send it hurtling into the valley
without harming Wren.
My thoughts rustled
from my leaves
and reached my sisters
who chorused
"No!
Sycamore says the man inside
has been friends with Wise Bramley
since he was a child.
He played under the boughs
of far Copper Beech
and freed tree huggers at Stonehenge!"
I heard the conflict in their voices.
They were frightened for me

but this decision came
from Sycamore Tree.

Round and round

The shadow passed repeatedly

right
to
left
to
right

"Fly away," I told Wren.
She had seen a spider
and disregarded my plea.
I shook to make her leave.
The spider scrabbled
behind moss,
retracted his legs into a ball
and hid.
I pleaded with Wren,
"You must flee!"
She pecked stubbornly.
Her tail ticked to and fro.
Green flecks scattered
over her claws
as the shadow grew
left
to
right

Wren continued,
oblivious.

the tree got bigger
and bigger

My sisters yelled
"What are you doing?
You need to get ready!"
"Wren won't leave."
"That's her look out,
do you want to lose your arms?"
Its movement tightened to a circle
right
left
centred
over
my
head

pivoting on its nose.
My sisters' anguish throbbed the air,
the shadow
darkened
my
crown.

Wind collided in vortexes,
swirled my leaves,
whirled down my trunk
and flurried Wren's wings.
She glanced up.
Her eyes popped
and she flit off
with the spider in her beak.

I dug down with my roots
and summoned sap
to make my boughs malleable.
I instructed my twigs
to weave a net
and leaves to overlap.
An eerie whistle pierced the sky.
For a fraction of a second
all was silent.

I took a deep breath

and opened my branches.

I hit the tree
that was waiting for me

The machine fell
wingtip first.

and then there were some noises,
branches breaking
because they'd been severed

Its edges cut like machetes.
My branches screamed
and seeped as their tips sheared off.
Leaves were chopped to pieces.
It took all my will
not to harden
against the wings

the glider hadn't stopped
at the point of entry

plunging down.
They flayed my bark
and gouged my flesh.
But I kept myself pliable.
I let the machine

sink

into my arms.

but it slowed and...

Freight juddered my bole
and engulfed my limbs.
My root hairs tremored.
Soil vibrated
at my feet
and worms writhed in tunnels.
Beetles gripped grit with their legs.
The wind machine came to a stop
where Wren
had caught the spider.

I exhaled.

The sole sound
was the purl of my sap
flowing back.
I was empty of birds
and the man in the machine
did not move.

It was too quiet.

My twigs peered at the man's face.
His eyes were closed.
They scratched the machine
and he did not wake.
They tapped near the man's head.
It was no use.

He was dead.

I hung my head in shame.
My branches trailed the ground.
I messaged my sisters, "I failed."
They did not reply.
My leaves shrivelled
and I sagged from my stem.

Wren returned
and raised her speckled wing
in a hug. I was inconsolable.
She hopped onto the
broken wind machine
and pecked its eye.
The sound amplified.
She drummed.
Each time her beak hit
her body bucked
and the beat reverberated.
The machine shook
from wing to wing,
nose to tail.
The branches cradling it shook too
and my leaves syncopated a beat.
Inside the machine
the man stirred.
His face tipped up.

My twigs cheered,
"He's alive!"
and my sisters messaged,
"We knew you could do it."
Sycamore growled,
"Have faith in yourself, my son,"
and I was proud

to be counted his kin.

...there I was.

In that tree.

If I'd gone into the ground,
I'd have been killed.

The tree saved me.

The glider was on its side
and I was sitting on my side
unable to get out.

I couldn't release my safety belt,
the one in front of my harness
because then I would have
gone straight to the ground
and probably killed myself.

so, I had the sense to stay put.

After a few seconds, perhaps
half a minute I heard two
men approaching me,
they shouted, "Awrrright?"
and I shouted, "Yes."
Not poachers but
agricultural workers,

they asked
"Do you want a ladder?"
I laughed, "Yes please."
I jolly well wasn't going to move
until I was safe to get down
to the ground.

It didn't take long
for the ladder to reach me

and that was the end

of my competition career.

And there we are.

Last year Wren domed her nest
in my fork.
She taught her children to fly.
Every time one fledged
she advised,
"If anyone comments on your size,

tell them
you come from the beech on the ridge
who caught a wind machine
and saved a human life."

I told my sisters this
and they smiled.

A Marriage in Chicklade Orchard

Wiltshire Times | 23 May 1995

On Saturday 21 May, the marriage took place between Jasmine Phillips, second daughter of Mr. and Mrs. Derek Phillips of Chicklade, and Mr. Edmund Clay, only son of Mr. and Mrs. Jonathan Clay of Fovant. The happy couple met at the archives of Bottlebrush Down where Edmund was researching his great grandfather's sighting of the Bronze Age Warrior.

The ceremony was conducted in the orchard at Chicklade. Guests reported that after the vows a gust of wind sprinkled petals on the newlyweds.

The End

Author's Note

I grew up in Wiltshire. Decades after leaving home I nearly died as a passenger in a car crash. I returned to the landscape of my childhood to recover. The downs and valleys soothed me. Fond memories revived.

My paternal grandmother, Jessie, shared our family home. The orchard was her favourite place. She reposed among trees, tilted her face to their canopies and listened. Sun danced on her freckles, her wrinkles softened and eyelids closed. Jessie suffered loss in her lifetime, but joy defined her. By the time I returned she had been dead for years. I pictured her in the countryside, exploring tumuli that dotted the fields. The ancient burial mounds were spiritual.

My favourite tumulus was round and covered with dense grass. I sat on it to watch the sun go down and connected with bones beneath. Others made similar connections. I met ghost hunters where two footpaths crossed near Bottlebrush Down[1]. They sought the Bronze Age warrior[2]. Respected archaeologist RCC Clay saw the spectre in 1924[3]. The horseman galloped alongside his vehicle for forty yards before vanishing, "by a low, round barrow." 'Barrow' is another word for tumulus.

I had been back in Wiltshire for a year when I asked Dad about his glider crash. He had not spoken of it before. My own near-death experience permitted me to raise the subject. Dad started talking and I knew he would tell it all. I hit record on my phone.

Dad cried as he recalled his plunge to death.

One sentence stood out,

"The tree was waiting for me."

I was shocked. Dad is a straightforward kind of guy. He is not prone to romancing anything let alone trees. It reminded me of Jessie in her orchard.

Dad's words took me back to the day of his crash. It was summer and I was a girl. I loitered under the airfield's control tower. Radioed talk escaped through open windows. White noise buzzed. I leant towards it. Crackles snapped. A voice stuttered, indecipherable. The crackles broke. Silence. Seconds passed. Crackles pounced back. A pilot gabbled,

"Mayday, mayday, mayday. Derek Phillips."

Dad's and my recollections of that day went round and round in my head.

His survival was a miracle. A question haunted me.

How come a tree saved Dad?

I could not find the answer, so I made one up. Jessie's friendship with trees was my inspiration. *Into My Arms* is set in Wiltshire because that's where we lived at the time of Dad's crash. I redrew Jessie's grief. Trees witnessed her mourn. It hurt them. They joined a pact to protect her son. I created adventures for Jessie in wilderness, folklore and nature. Her reimagined life arrived at Brother Beech who caught my dad.

Into My Arms fictionalizes family, names and occupations. Characters and events are unreal. The Bronze Age Warrior is real to me.

The essence of Jessie is true. Dad's words are true. The love is true.

Postscript

The journey of *Into My Arms* continues. I am preparing a multimedia performance tour of the titular work.

1 January 2026

---

[1] *A stone's throw away in neighbouring Dorset.*

[2] *"Horseman" South West England The Paranormal Database, https://www.paranormaldatabase.com/dorset/dorsdata.php?pageNum_paradata=13a*

The Spectral Horseman, Haunted Britain and Ireland https://www.haunted-britain.com/bottlebush-down.htm

[3] *The Phantom Horseman of Bottlebrush Down, 18.5.2010 Fairweather Lewis https://fairweatherlewis.wordpress.com/2010/05/18/the-phantom-horseman-of-bottlebrush-down/*

Research

"Mother Trees share their excess carbon and nitrogen through the mycorrhizal network with the understory seedlings, which can increase seedling survival."

About Mother Trees in the Forest, The Mother Tree Project and Programme

https://mothertreeproject.org/about-mother-trees-in-the-forest/

"He [David Haskell] *found trees do communicate. They communicate with the soil, the weather, other living creatures, and yes, they send out pulses like the vibrations of our vocal cords."*

WGLT (2017) 'Biologist Studies the Voices (And Songs) of Trees' 2 October 2017

"If a giraffe starts eating an African Acacia, the tree releases chemicals into the air that signals a threat is at hand. As the chemical drifts through the air and reaches other trees, they 'smell' it and are warned of danger."/ "If a tree falls in the forest there are other trees listening..."

(Foreword Tim Flannery /central theme) Wohlleben, P. (2017) The Hidden Life of Trees, William Collins

"...the assumption that electrical signals ...trigger rapid leaf movements in ... ordinary plants proved to be correct."

From, J. and Lautner, S. 2007. Abstract:- 'Electrical Signals and Their Physiological Significance in Plants' National Center for Biotechnology Information, National Library of Medicine, USA.

https://pubmed.ncbi.nlm.nih.gov/17263772/

"The necessity for plants to having developed networks of electrical signalling is most likely due to enable rapid response to environmental stimuli and stress factors."

Galle, A., Lautner, S., Flexas, J., and Fromm, J. (2015). Introduction 'Environmental Stimuli and Physiological Responses: The Current View on Electrical Signalling.' Environmental and Experimental Botany, Elsevier, Science Direct. Volume 114, June 2015, pp. 15-21.

https://www.sciencedirect.com/science/article/abs/pii/S0098847214001634

"Thirsty or damaged plants produce up to 50 staccato pops in an hour, which nearby creatures may respond to, researchers find... 'When these

plants are in good shape, they produce less than one sound per hour, but when stressed they emit many more, sometimes 30 to 50 per hour' (Prof. Lilach Hadany) [...] At 40 to 80 kHz, the sounds are too high-pitched for the human ear, which has an upper range of about 20 kHz. But insects such as moths and small mammals including mice can detect such frequencies ..."

Sample, I. (2023) 'Plants emit ultrasonic sounds in rapid bursts when stressed, scientists say' The Guardian, 30 March referencing Khait, I., Lewin-Epstein, O., Sharon, R., Sade, N., Yovel, Y., and Hadany, L. 'Sounds Emitted By Plants Under Stress Are Airborne and Informative'
https://www.theguardian.com/environment/2023/mar/30/plants-emitultrasonic-sounds-in-rapid-bursts-when-stressed-scientists-say

"Trees also communicate through the air, using pheromones and other scent signals."

Grant, R. (2018) 'Do Trees Talk To Each Other?' Smithsonian Magazine
https://www.smithsonianmag.com/science-nature/the-whispering-trees-180968084/

"Willow contains plant compounds including populin and methyl salicylates. Populin is also found in cottonwood and contributes to both trees species' anti-inflammatory and fever reducing medicine. Methyl salicylates have a minty or wintergreen smell."

GoodGrub, (9 November 2023) 'Plant of the Month: Willow'
https://www.goodgrub.org/post/plant-of-the-month-willow

"...conifers are ready to harvest in around forty years..." and "we may well have felled some 66,000 acres of Britain's rainforests in the twentieth century alone... and all in the name of planting trees for timber..."

Shrubsole, G. (2022) The Lost Rainforests of Britain, pp.159 and 163

The Great War (1914-1918) is how World War I (WWI) was known

"During the war years of 1914 to 1918, Britain was mostly cut off from its overseas timber supplies and had to rely on its own forests for timber."

Landscape Ecol (2020) pp. 2715. Land-Use Legacies of Twentieth-Century Forestry in the UK: A Perspective. Susanne Raum, Springer Nature.

https://doi.org/10.1007/s10980-020-01126-1

"By 1918, 182,000 hectares of woodland had been felled – an area larger than modern-day Greater London... By 1919, woodland cover was at an all-time low of 5%..."

9 September 2019 'History of Britain's forests and woodlands: 100 years of the Forestry Commission' BBC Countryfile.

https://www.countryfile.com/wildlife/trees-plants/history-of-britains-forests-and-woodlands-celebrating-100-years-of-the-forestry-commission

"During the First World War... The native woodlands were felled on a gigantic scale with most of the best trees being removed. The woods did not have time to recover, nor had the newly created coniferous forests become productive before the Second World War resulted in a repeat of the onslaught. The only trees left behind were generally small and badly formed."

Future Trees Trust: Broadleaved Woodland and the Need for Tree Breeding" in 'History of Our Forests.

https://www.futuretrees.org/about-us/history-of-our-forests/

In the period 1972-95 there were 76 fatalities in the UK from gliding accidents, *"...failing to recognize when they are approaching the point of no return for continued safe flight is a constant hazard for all pilots, regardless of their age and experience."* (The Air Accidents Investigation Branch).

The Battle of The Beanfield took place on 1 June 1985. More than 500 New Age Travellers were arrested in what was one of the largest mass arrests since the Second World War. Derek Phillips was a lawyer. He procured the release for the majority of the travellers wrongly incarcerated at Salisbury police station. Six years later, a court found the police guilty of wrongful arrest, assault and criminal damage.

Ares is the Greek god of war renowned for his accuracy with a bow and arrow.

Chapters of *Into My Arms* previously published, performed and exhibited:

The Bride was written for the National Trust and performed at National Trust Kingston Lacy for Blossom Week 2024. A photo poem of *The Bride* was included in the Biophilia exhibition at Dorchester Hospital created by Dorset Visual Arts with The Arborealists in 2025. Biophilia subsequently toured. This tour extended into 2026.

The Headless Horseman was commissioned by Cranborne Chase National Landscape, and Chase & Chalke as a headline performance piece at the Festival of Words in 2023.

Further performances took place at The Larmer Tree Gardens in 2024. Cranborne Chase National Landscape and Chase & Chalke published the work in a stand-alone pamphlet the same year. This piece was also performed at Swindon Festival of Literature's 2025 finale, and Chalke History Festival in 2025.

Acknowledgements

Thank you to Ed, Matt, Chris, Cat and Rose at Road Song Books for your care and attention in the publication of Into My Arms. It has been a wonderful experience. Thank you for your dedication, expertise and a stunning cover. The strength of Road Song's teamwork is a privilege I have enjoyed. Ed, you have been fantastic throughout. I cannot thank you enough.

In my work, I owe thanks to a great many people. This acknowledgment relates to *Into My Arms*. Its route to publication has been via paper and stage. Thank you everyone who shared its journey.

Thank you, Literature Works for a brilliant year on your Word Space Talent Development programme, as well as Miriam Darlington and Jon Woolcott for their superb mentoring and partnership. I learned a lot and met great writers.

I am indebted to Jawbone Collective, for their selfless dedication and support of writers and poets. I thank Peter Roe and Megan Simson. You dignified me when I crumbled. I will never forget your kindness. Thank you also Izzy Robertson and Clare Morris.

Thank you to Cranborne Chase National Landscape, Chase & Chalke and the wondrous Charlotte Moreton. Thank you, Dominic Wong at the fabulous Bournemouth Writing Festival, Amy Juliet Brown at Winchester Poetry Festival, Chalke History Festival, National Trust Kingston Lacy, Finola Brennan and Nat Wood Fox at Blandford Literary Festival, also Matt Holland at Swindon Festival of Literature.

Thank you, Sue Kinnear at BBC Radio Wiltshire.

Thank you, Paul Newman at Dorset Visual Arts, The Arborealists, and Arts in Hospitals, especially Suzy Rushbrook.

A big thank you to Tom Bromley of Salisbury Writers Circle for years of knowledge, wisdom and generosity in helping writers. You give so much. Your teaching shaped this work. Thank you also Christine Nielsen-Craig.

I thank Barney Norris for being an inspiration and an example. For creating the space in which *Into My Arms* developed, thank you to Andy Buchanan, MAST Southampton, Artful Scribe, Susmita Bhattacharya, Abby G Poetree, the Russell-Cotes Museum, Millie Woodrow and Close Poetry. Thank you June Cluett for her rural platform at Wyle Valley Writers and Sam Holland-Bunyan for the stage at St Peter's Church, Fugglestone.

Thank you, Frankie Sinclair for so much. I thank Niky Harris for her encouragement and others at Poetica, especially Edwin Hopper and John Bruce. Closer to home, thank you Mikaela and Roger Boon, Allen Chalke, Karen and Simon Allsebrook, Miranda Dobbs and Julia Thomas. Thank you to the Revd Alison Waterhouse for sharing your faith. Thank you to the Church of all Saints, Broad Chalke.

To those of you who read and commented on *Into My Arms*, I appreciate the selfless gift of your time. Thank you, Angela McAllister, Barney Norris, Ben Goldsmith, David Gladwin, Derek Gow, Jeff Young, Mark McDonald, Mark Wigan, Nat Wood Fox, Paul Wood, and Tim Craven.

Thank you to my family and friends and Broad Chalke village.

I thank the trees for saving Dad.

Thank you, Simmy for goofy love.

Thank you, Mum and Dad.

Last and most I thank my beautiful children Angus, Chris, Sam and Jessie.

Estelle, 6 January 2026

Road Song Books would like to thank the Bideford Bridge Trust for their start-up grant which enabled us to invite fine authors such as Estelle to collaborate on their writing projects. We would also like to thank all the generous writers who have taken time out to preview and offer reviews for our book covers. Thanks especially to everybody that reads, buys and stocks our books. The writers that submit manuscripts to us – we see you. Finally, thanks are due to the members of the Indie Publishing Network and David Gladwin.

Also published by Road Song Books

The Magpie by Alan Edward Roberts
A Century of Storms by Alan Edward Roberts
Cerberus by Alan Edward Roberts
Coldwell by David Gladwin
Gentle November by Alan Edward Roberts